the Lovesick SKUNK

By Joe Hayes
Illustrated by Antonio Castro L.

Cinco Puntos Press
www.cincopuntos.com

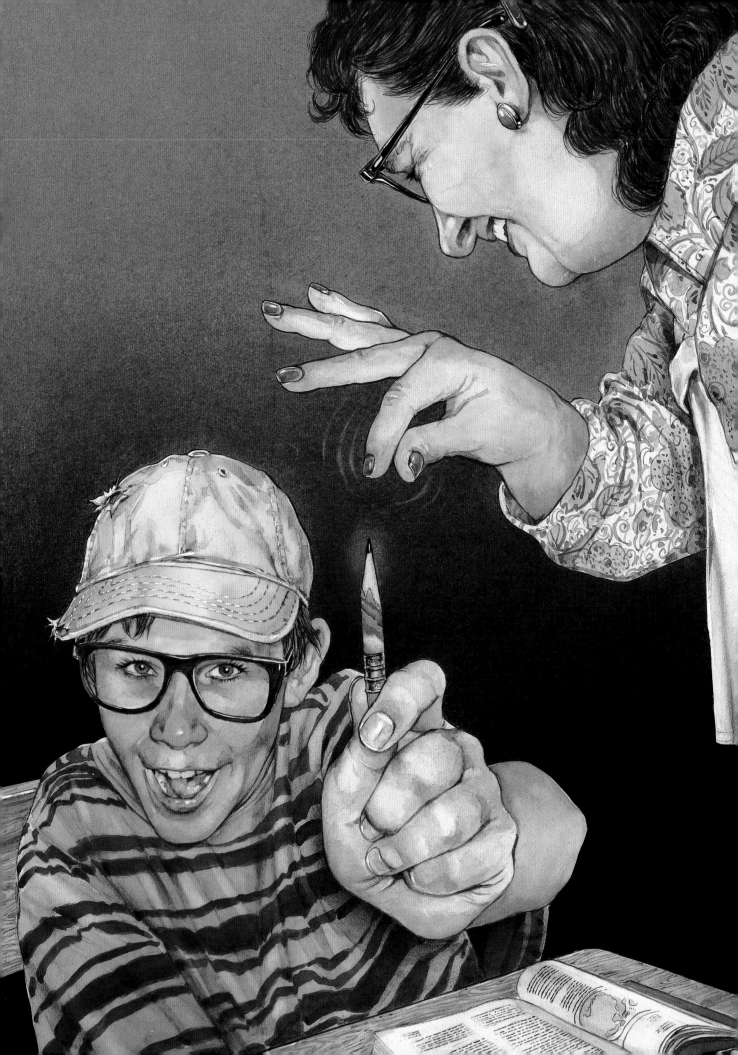

When I was a kid, I would get stuck on some simple little thing I really loved and never want to get rid of it or trade it for anything else. It might be a hat that felt just right on my head. Or a tee-shirt I'd wear until it was falling apart. Or even a favorite pencil.

Once I had a pencil with bright-colored stripes spiraling all around it—red, purple and green—with silver sparkles mixed in. The eraser was electric orange. I was the only kid in my class who had a pencil like that. I sharpened it until it got so tiny my teacher said I'd have to hold it with tweezers. "If you sharpen it any more," she said, "it's going to make invisible writing."

And once I had a pair of jeans I wore until they were so full of holes my friends called them my Swiss cheese pants. I didn't throw them away until my mom showed me they were about to get a hole in a pretty embarrassing place.

But I think the thing I loved the most was a pair of black and white sneakers. They were black high-top sneakers with a white stripe that kind of curved up from the toe to the top on each side. No one else had sneakers like mine.

I wore those shoes to school every day and to play in after school. I wore them all day long on the weekends. I wore them to birthday parties and ball games. If my mom had let me, I would have worn them to bed. And the more I wore them, the better they felt on my feet.

By the time summer came around, the laces had been broken and knotted at least twenty-five times. The sides were all tattered. One of them had a big hole in the bottom. But there was no way I would throw them away.

Every day in the summer, I'd wake up in the morning, jump back into the clothes I'd worn the day before and put on those beat up old black and white sneakers. I'd gulp down a quick bowl of cereal and head off into the desert with my good buddy Billy.

We'd spend the whole day wandering around through the mesquite and cactus or tromping through the mud and quicksand down by the little trickle of a river that ran close to our town.

Every day my black and white sneakers came home in worse shape.

But the worst thing about them was the smell! Your feet get really sweaty running around in the desert. And one day when we were running across a pasture, I stepped in a cow pie. That's not a pie cows like to eat. It's something that comes out the other end of a cow! That sure didn't make my shoes smell any better.

Another time my foot sank in some nasty smelling mud down by the river.

One day my mom met me at the door when I came home for supper. "You are not coming into this house with those shoes on," she declared and she made me take them off and leave them outside on the step.

My shoes were banned from the house, but do you think I stopped wearing them?

No way!

My mom bought me a new pair of black and white sneakers, just like the ones I loved. They even came from the same store. But I knew those shoes wouldn't feel the same. I didn't even try them on.

I didn't really understand how terrible my shoes smelled until the night Billy and I decided to camp out.

We had been wandering around down by the river that day and noticed a nice, grassy spot under a big cottonwood tree. We could see a circle of stones where someone had made a fire. It looked like a perfect campsite. It put the idea of a camp-out into our heads.

We headed home and asked our moms for permission and they both said it would be all right.

We packed up our sleeping bags and tent, some hotdogs and a can of beans to cook for supper, and a few odds and ends like a flashlight and some old silverware, and headed off on our big adventure.

It was already getting a little late when we got back to that big, shady tree. We pitched our tent and made a little fire in the stone circle. We cooked our supper and ate. After sitting around and poking the fire with sticks for a while, we got sleepy.

We poured water on the fire and then climbed into the tent. By that time I'd gotten used to leaving my shoes outside, so when I took them off I set them on the ground in front of the tent flap. We were pretty tired so we fell asleep right way.

But late at night I was awakened by a noise outside the tent, over by the fire circle. I found my flashlight on the floor of the tent and pointed the light over toward the fire pit. Two bright little lights came shining back at me— the eyes of some critter. And then I made out a plump black and white body. It was a skunk! A chubby little skunk.

Just about the time I shined the light on it, the skunk lost interest in whatever it was investigating over by the dead fire and started walking toward the tent. I reached over and shook Billy and he got up. We both sat there staring as the skunk got closer and closer to our tent. We were afraid to move. And then, just when it got to the door, the skunk turned around. Its tail end was pointing right at us.

We were expecting the worst!

But then we realized that what made the skunk turn around had nothing to do with us. The little skunk sidled over to my old black and white sneakers and laid its head on one of them. And then it started rubbing its cheek against them.

"Oh, my gosh," Billy whispered, "the skunk's falling in love with your smelly old shoes!"

Sure enough, the skunk started making the sweetest little purring sound—almost like a kitten—and began snuggling and cuddling up with my sneakers.

Billy and I crouched in the back of the tent staring, our mouths hanging open. We were trapped. It looked like we'd have to spend the whole night watching that skunk nuzzle against my smelly old shoes.

But a few minutes later, we noticed another movement over by the edge of the bushes. I shined the light over that way and there was another skunk. This one was huge. It was almost as big as my grandma's cocker spaniel. It came marching straight over to the black and white sneakers, pushed the lovey-dovey skunk aside and bit the toe of one of my shoes.

Then the big skunk turned around and—pssssst!—it sprayed my shoes!

The big skunk gave the little skunk the meanest look you ever saw and then turned and walked away. And my shoes' new girlfriend tagged along behind it.

My friend whispered, "That must be the little skunk's boyfriend."

Billy and I grabbed our sleeping bags in our arms and ran out of the tent holding our noses. When we got to where the smell wasn't so bad, we rolled out the bags again but we didn't get much sleep that night.

In the morning my shoes were so stinky not even I could stand them.

I waited there in my bare feet while Billy hiked back to my house to get me the new shoes my mom had bought. Then we packed everything up and headed for home. I turned and took one last, sad look at my good old sneakers. I promised myself I'd never forget them.

When I got home, my mom

didn't even ask me what happened to the old shoes. She was probably so happy to see I'd finally abandoned them that she really didn't care why.

Or maybe she knew that if she asked me, I'd just come up with some wild, unbelievable story—like a run-in with a lovesick skunk and her jealous boyfriend.

FIRST EDITION

10 9 8 7 6 5 4 3 2 1

Library of Congress Cataloging-in-Publication Data

Hayes, Joe.
 The lovesick skunk / by Joe Hayes ; illustrated by Antonio Castro L. — 1st ed.
   p. cm.
 Summary: A boy who likes to wear his favorite clothes constantly, no matter what, leaves his smelly, black and white sneakers outside his tent during a campout and witnesses their effect on a passing skunk.
 ISBN 978-1-933693-81-1 (alk. paper)
 [1. Sneakers—Fiction. 2. Clothing and dress—Fiction. 3. Skunks—Fiction. 4. Camping—Fiction. 5. Tall tales.] I. Castro López, Antonio, ill. II. Title.

PZ7.H31474Lov 2010
[E]--dc22

2010014617

Book and cover design by Antonio Castro H.

Printed in Hong Kong.